# The Cats Nobody Wanted

# The Cats Nobody Wanted

## Harriet May Savitz

AN
**APPLE**
PAPERBACK

SCHOLASTIC INC.
New York Toronto London Auckland Sydney

ISBN 0-590-42196-4

12 11 10 9 8 7 6 5 4 3 2 1          9/8 0 1 2 3 4/9

Printed in the U.S.A.                                   28

First Scholastic Printing, November 1989

*My gratitude to Sylvia Outland,
who never turns a cat
away from her door;
Robert Laliberte; Fabio Doug Battaglia;
and Todd Laliberte.*

*A special thanks to Ina and Jerry Luber.*

# The Cats Nobody Wanted

# 1

The first time I met the cat lady, I was just walking by the big green-and-white house on my way to school. I didn't even know she lived there. I knew someone lived there because I had seen a moving van in the driveway the week before. The day I walked by, I noticed some white paper plates on the front brick steps, one on each step leading up to the front door. There was some food on the plates as if someone were expected for breakfast.

While I stood there wondering whom the food was for, I got the feeling I was being watched. I looked up toward the front porch. A cat was sitting at the window, looking out at me from the inside. His brown body was hunched up the way cats get when they're taking a nap. His white nose was pressed against the windowpane.

But that wasn't the only cat watching me. There was another one in the window on the other side of the porch — a black cat with bright green eyes.

I looked up to the first floor of the house and my mouth dropped open. There was a cat looking out from just about every window in the house, and there were plenty of windows. One cat was grey; another, bright orange; another, striped. I guess there must have been eight cats staring down at me from the green-and-white house.

Were there more cats? I wondered. I walked up the driveway to the backyard. I wasn't too surprised to find a puffy white cat sitting on a picnic table. While I was standing there, a cat bigger than any I had ever seen ran between my legs.

"What are you looking at, young man?" a lady asked as she took her broom and began sweeping the back porch. "Do you want a cat?"

We had never had a pet in our house and I didn't think my parents would want one now. Lately, they didn't seem to need anything but Greta, my new baby sister.

"I just was wondering where all these cats came from," I answered. "Do you own all of them?"

"You don't own a cat." The lady smiled as if I had said something silly. "A cat owns you. I'm just taking care of these for a while. They were abused cats. People had not taken care of them properly. Whenever I find abandoned cats, I take them home and care for them until they're adopted."

We sat down on her back steps. There were two kittens playing in front of us. The lady placed a black-and-white one in my lap. She held a pure black one with large blue eyes.

"These two just came in yesterday. I found them under the porch over there." She pointed to the house across the street. "They were left by their mother and in a few weeks would have gone wild. I was afraid they'd get hit by a car."

When I finally left the cat lady's house, I could still feel the kitten purring as I stroked him. I asked my friend Denny about the cat lady later that day.

"Do you want to go over there with me tomorrow?" I said.

"Not me," he answered, tossing me the basketball in his driveway. "I'm allergic to animals. Besides, my mom said Mrs. Beasley is getting people angry with her. Her cats sometimes get out of the house and run into the neighbors' gardens."

I didn't think that was such a terrible thing. It was better than having the cats starving in the cold and left to die.

Every day I made it my business to pass Mrs. Beasley's house on my way to school. There were always paper plates outside and cats inside staring out the windows. Every day I thought more and more about owning one of those cats.

I tried bringing the subject up to my mother, but she didn't have the time to listen.

"Honey, I'll be with you in a minute," she'd say. "Greta needs me right now. Is it important?"

It was getting more and more important to me as I spent more and more time sitting on Mrs. Beasley's front porch, talking to the cats through the window, or sitting on the back steps, playing with the cats she had let out in the backyard. I learned there was one thing about a cat you couldn't do and that was fence him in. Most of the houses on our block had fenced-in backyards for their dogs. But when I sat in Mrs. Beasley's backyard, I just watched the cats leap high over all the fences in front of them. It was as if they had wings and knew nothing could stop them from being free.

"Do you want to help me feed and groom them?" the cat lady asked when she found me staring up at her window one day after school. There was a particular cat that had my attention. She was grey with a white stripe down her nose, and every time I talked to her from the front porch, she stood up and scratched against the windowpane as if she were trying to reach me.

"I sure would," I answered.

4

I followed Mrs. Beasley around to the backyard. She took a comb and brush from a wooden box resting on the back steps. "Just hold their front paws gently, pressing them against you, and comb them." One by one, Mrs. Beasley brought a cat out from the house. She watched as I combed each one. Mrs. Beasley talked to the cat as I combed it.

"There you are, Bella. Nice and safe now. No one will mistreat you ever again. I'll see to that. Only the best home and family for you."

Finally it was Grey's turn. "Where did Grey come from?" I asked. It seemed the most natural name for her, since there wasn't another color on her except the thin white line down her nose.

"She was thrown from a truck," Mrs. Beasley explained. "I remember that rainy day very well. I saw this ball come flying from the driver's side and then I found her, curled up by the side of the road, wet, and shaking, almost in shock. You see, she still has that little limp."

I held on tightly to Grey, wanting her to feel loved and not alone.

"She had lost her dignity that day," Mrs. Beasley continued. "A cat has to have her dignity in order to live a quality life. You see, you are giving her that back right now, Frankie. Combing her, giving her love . . ."

Grey must have understood Mrs. Beasley because she nestled in my arms. I could almost see her fur taking on a shine as I brushed her.

Just then, a man about Mrs. Beasley's age came out from her house.

"All done napping, Jimmy?" Mrs. Beasley asked. "Can you pick me up some cat food next time you go to the grocery store?"

"Gotcha," Jimmy said. He pulled at his blue suspenders as he walked by.

"Jimmy lives next door," Mrs. Beasley explained. "He helps me out and I help him out. His memory isn't too good these days. He doesn't have any family living around him and neither do I. Except for my cats."

I wanted to tell someone about the fun I was having at the cat lady's house. I tried with Denny but he wasn't interested. "All you want to talk about anymore is cats, Frankie." Then he pushed me into the pile of fall leaves and we rolled down the hill in front of my house. It was fun, but not as much fun as playing with Grey.

I tried telling my parents about the cat lady, but they had company in to see Greta. Everyone was standing around her crib, oohing and aahing. They were making a big fuss about her skin. "It's just like peaches and cream," said Mrs. Berry, from up the street. "And her hair. Look how thick and dark it is."

My hair is thick and dark but no one seemed to care. Later, when everyone left, I went into Greta's bedroom and stared down at her, wondering how anyone so small could cause so much commotion in one house. She was always crying for something to eat, or there was usually a wet diaper to change. When she wasn't hungry, she was sleeping. I don't know why, but everyone who visited thought that was cute. They'd stare down at her and smile, even when her eyes were closed. I tiptoed from the room so I wouldn't wake her. Even though she lived in my house, I felt like I didn't know her, and I knew she didn't know me, either.

# 2

Grandpop Willie's letter came the next day. It was waiting for me on the kitchen table. I opened it real fast because Grandpop always made me feel better about everything.

"*Dear Frankie,*" the letter read. "*Can't you write anymore, son? It's been two weeks and no letter. What are you, too busy for this old man? You jumping around in the fall leaves or playing basketball?*

"*I've been busy with my stamp collection. This week I went to a stamp show and bought some old Presidential series with the pictures of Washington, Madison, and John Adams on the stamps. Now, that's a real prize.*

"*If it's not too much trouble, Frankie, drop me a note. Your fingers won't break off when you pick up the pencil. I promise. Love, Gramps.*"

It was a great letter. Grandpop Willie didn't mention Greta once. I ran upstairs to answer him right away. I felt bad that I had been so busy with Mrs. Beasley's cats, I had forgotten about Gramps. Grandpop looked forward to my letters. That was the only way we got to talk to one another. He hated the telephone.

"You can't keep a telephone conversation in a scrapbook or take it out in a year and reread it like a letter," he'd say.

He had been writing to me since I was old enough to print my name. He always told me you could write the truth in a letter as long as you had someone on the other side you could trust. I trusted Grandpop Willie, so I told him just how I felt about Greta.

*"It's Greta this and Greta that. I tell you, Grandpop, you'd think no one else lived in this house."*

And then I told him about the cat lady, Mrs. Beasley, and Grey. *"She's such a gentle cat,"* I wrote. *"She needs a home with a lot of love. I know she feels I love her. I can tell by the way she purrs when I hold her."* I signed the letter, addressed the envelope, and grabbed a stamp from the top of my dad's desk in his study. Then I ran down to the corner mailbox and dropped the letter in the slot. For a moment, I felt better about everything because I always had Grandpop Willie to share my problems with.

But the next day I got that lonely feeling again. Nobody seemed to care when I walked in or out of the house. For the next couple of weeks, I could have fallen into a large hole and disappeared. I doubted if anyone would have missed me.

Usually, when it rained, my mom would remind me to wear my raincoat and hat when I went out. But it rained practically a whole week and she was so busy burping Greta and changing diapers, she didn't even notice the raindrops covering our windows. I had to remember my coat and hat all by myself.

Another thing that made me grumpy was missing my sleepovers with Denny. On Friday night, he usually slept over my house. Sometimes we swapped baseball cards. Most of the time we read jokebooks until real late. After my mom turned out the bedroom lamps, we'd turn our flashlights on and read under the blankets. Denny had missed three Friday nights already. One weekend he had a cold. The other two weekends his parents were having company and when I asked if he could come to my house, my mom said, "Wait a while, Frankie. The noise might wake the baby up. You and Denny are not the quietest people." She was smiling when she said it and she kissed me on the cheek, but it didn't make me feel any better.

In the meantime, because no one seemed to care where I was lately as long as I tiptoed through the house when Greta was sleeping, I spent a lot of time at the cat lady's house. I watched her give the cats their medicine, and she even taught me how to give them pills. She'd hold a cat's paws while I slid the pill behind his tongue, and when he swallowed, it wound up down his throat. Sometimes she gave a stubborn cat medicine through a dropper.

There were always chores to do around Mrs. Beasley's house and she made me feel that she needed my help to do them. We changed the kitty litter pans every two days. There were food dishes to fill or wash out, and fresh water bowls to put on the floor. And when the chores were finished, the fun time came. I'd sit and hold Grey and brush her hair while Jimmy sat in the rocking chair, snoring, usually with a cat sleeping in his lap.

One day I was there when a family came to adopt a cat. A girl about my age stood in Mrs. Beasley's living room with her father. Mrs. Beasley let the girl hold the cat she wanted. The cat's name was Summer because Mrs. Beasley had found her in July.

"You have to give Summer plenty of love," Mrs. Beasley told the girl. "She likes to have her back scratched gently, and remember to keep her well fed and to brush her now and then."

"I will," the girl promised.

I told Grandpop Willie in my next letter about all the work I was doing at Mrs. Beasley's house. Then I told him where all the cat food came from.

*"Mrs. Beasley buys a lot of it herself,"* I wrote him. *"She has some people who donate money and food. But every day, there's a new cat living there. And if no one adopts them, Mrs. Beasley takes them to a veterinarian to have them fixed so they cannot have kittens and multiply. She says that would be cruel, having kittens starve. Then she puts the cats back in their natural environment. If they came from the woods, she returns them there. She says that's better than destroying them because older cats have a better chance of getting their own food."*

I told Grandpop Willie he'd like the cat lady. Mrs. Beasley always had time to tell me about her day and to listen while I told her about mine. There wasn't any time at my house to tell stories. But Mrs. Beasley always had a story to tell about a new cat and where it came from. Sometimes when I was talking to my parents, they'd be cooking dinner, or running around the kitchen putting dishes away. Mrs. Beasley never did work when she listened. She'd just sit there right next to me and look straight at me when I talked, as if everything I said was very important.

"I can't believe that woman has so many cats," my mother said one day when we were taking Greta for a walk in the carriage. "I hear her neighbors on the block aren't too happy about it. The cats are knocking over the trash cans. I think they'd be very happy if she just got rid of all her cats."

"That's how much they know," I said, straining to see if Grey was looking out a window. "Mrs. Beasley said cats can get rid of mice and they have a soothing effect on people. They're great companions. If more people adopted them, the cat lady wouldn't have so many cats."

I was hoping Mrs. Beasley didn't know what was going on around her, but I could tell by her face that she did the next time I visited her. She usually had this bright smile, but that day she wasn't singing when she groomed the cats. She didn't talk much when we fed them. Finally she sat down on the couch. She pushed her curly white hair away from her eyes. I sat down next to her. Grey jumped on my lap as she usually did when

I came to call. She was beginning to spend all her time with me. Lately I was thinking of her as my cat anyway.

"I don't know what gets into people," the cat lady finally said. "These cats are the gentlest creatures." She shook her head. "Who else would sit and listen to you without complaining? Such loyal friends. Frankie, I think I'm going to have to find another place to live. This is about the third time I've moved in just a few years. I don't know why, but it makes people uncomfortable to know I have so many cats living with me. Some of the neighbors already are showing up at the township meetings complaining about me and my family. You know, most of my cats stay inside. It's only one or two that get out now and then. But I guess many people don't have much understanding about animals. I'm going to have to move on if the complaints continue."

"You can't do that." I just about jumped up off the couch. Grey flew in the air, her tail thick, her fur standing straight up as if I had frightened her. Even Jimmy opened his eyes for a couple of moments before he nodded back to sleep in the rocking chair. "You can't just move away," I said. "What would happen to Jimmy?" Actually, what I was thinking was, What would happen to Grey and Mrs. Beasley? How would we see each other?

I couldn't imagine not visiting Grey. Even though she didn't live in my house, I considered her mine, and I know she didn't want to belong to anyone else.

Mrs. Beasley just nodded her head. We didn't talk much during the rest of my visit. I just held Grey tightly and hoped that my parents weren't going to the township meetings and complaining along with everyone else in the neighborhood.

I had to ask my parents that, face to face. "You're not one of those people trying to get rid of Mrs. Beasley's cats, are you?" I asked when I got home.

My mother looked up from the stack of clothes she was folding. "No, I'm not, Frankie, though I can't blame some of the people who live closer to her. The cats keep getting loose and they run through their backyards."

My dad split in half the apple he was eating and handed me a piece. "What brought this up, Frankie?"

"The cat lady might move because of all the complaints. I think it's mean of everyone when all she is doing is giving cats back their dignity."

My dad looked sort of surprised when I said that, as if I had told him something he had never heard before. "Look, Frankie, not everyone loves animals the way Mrs. Beasley does. What you do in your house sometimes spills over and affects the people who live around you.

"But no, in answer to your question, we aren't part of the group showing up at the township meetings." Then he kissed me on the head and took out a deck of cards so we could play War.

Though it made me feel a little better, I had another question I wanted to ask, the one that started, "There's this grey cat, and she has a way of putting her head right under my chin and purring real soft, and we belong together. Can I bring her home, because she was abused and left to starve, and she would be grateful for a place to sleep that's warm and for two meals a day?"

But that question stuck inside me and wouldn't come out. It stayed there during the card game and it took away the happiness I usually felt when Dad and I played War. It stayed with me each time I stood in front of our house and looked down the block toward the cat lady's house on the corner. It stayed with me at night before I went to bed, when I stood in my pajamas, looking out the window toward Mrs. Beasley's windows. From my house I could see her top floor, and sometimes I could just about see a cat's face looking out. But somehow I just couldn't ask my parents about Grey. It was one of those questions that had to be asked at just the right time.

# 3

Come on," said the cat lady the next time I came to call. "We're going on a roundup. Go home and ask your mother if you can come. We'll be about an hour or two, and I don't want your mother to worry."

I ran right home. Mom was busy bathing Greta when I rushed into the room. "Get me that towel, will you, Frankie?" she asked.

I ran over to the stack of soft white towels and handed her one. "The cat lady wants me to go with her this morning," I told my mom. "She has some things she needs to do and she wants me to keep her company."

For some reason I left out the good part about the cat roundup. I didn't think my mom would appreciate Mrs. Beasley bringing home more cats.

"You know you have your Saturday chores to do," my mom said. She had that "it better be done today" look on her face. Lately I wasn't doing much of anything I was expected to do. I had a

17

lot on my mind. One of the things was the giggling baby sister who was kicking up her feet and reaching for my fingers. I let them slip into her soft hand and she began pulling at them.

"I'll clean up my room as soon as I get back. I promise," I said. "And I'll even rake up the leaves this afternoon." I was willing to promise anything just so I could go on the roundup.

"Okay, Frankie," my mom said, but she didn't look too happy about it. "I'm going to hold you to your promise."

The roundup began at the supermarket. Mrs. Beasley pulled her station wagon over into the parking lot. "People always leave cats back here," she said. "And the cats seem to hang around because they know they'll find food. I've been leaving some in a cage way in the back of the lot, so no one can see it but the cats. It takes a while for them to trust you. Sometimes I leave one of the traps in a secluded place for days. Those cats are smart. They walk around it, and even though they might be starving, sometimes they just won't bite the bait."

Today there was one trap. The cat lady and I knelt far enough away from it so that we couldn't be seen. It was a cage, really, and inside was a plate of cat food. The door to the cage was open. We sat like that for quite a while, just waiting. I never had this much fun when I went to the supermarket with my parents.

I guess we waited for about a half hour. I wondered if we looked strange, kneeling like that for so long. I didn't think too many people would think it would be worth it, just to catch some cats. I was beginning to wonder if it was worth it myself when Mrs. Beasley nudged me.

"Look at those bushes. Did you see them move? We've got something coming out. We might be lucky today and actually see a cat go after the food."

Sure enough, in a couple of minutes, a kitten ran out from the bushes toward the cage. The very light brown kitten looked around, then walked around the cage, then looked to the right and the left.

"Don't move," Mrs. Beasley whispered.

I concentrated on being very still. The kitten was having a hard time making up her mind about the food inside the cage. Finally I guess her hunger got the best of her. Slowly she walked toward it. The trapdoor snapped shut behind her.

"We've got her!" Mrs. Beasley jumped up and ran toward the cage. "That's a good little girl, Puff," the cat lady said to the kitten that looked like a puffball. Her voice was very gentle when she spoke. "We're going to bring you home to join our family."

19

She handed me the cage to carry as we hurried back to the station wagon. Back at the house, Puff was introduced to the rest of the gang. The kitten didn't look like any of the other cats Mrs. Beasley kept at her house. She was dirty, with bits of grass stuck to her fur. I could feel the bones through her skin, and she was shaking in my lap as I held her.

"Here, Frankie. You comb her gently, now. This kitten needs to get back her dignity. The poor thing would have starved to death if we hadn't got her soon."

I wasn't certain how to handle Puff because she was the first cat I had brought home from a round-up. Mrs. Beasley noticed.

"Don't worry, Frankie. Puff isn't a scratcher yet. She hasn't gone wild. Look at the poor thing — she's shaking right out of her fur."

I was very careful not to frighten the kitten even more. I talked to her the way Mrs. Beasley did while I combed her fur and cleaned her off with a damp rag. Finally she had a little shine to her coat. Then the cat lady put Puff into a very large cage that had a plate of food and water, and a small box filled with kitty litter.

"I'll just keep her in there for a few days," she explained. "When she gets used to using the litter and to her new surroundings, I'll let her out to mix with her new family."

*    *    *

The next day when I went to visit, Puff was using the kitty litter in the box. After she ate her meal, she cleaned herself.

"She's a smart one," Mrs. Beasley said. She turned the pages of the little red telephone book she used when trying to find a family to adopt a cat. "I'd better let our group know we have a new kitten to adopt out," she said. "The Friends of Cats work very hard looking for the right homes."

Grey didn't seem to like the idea that I was paying so much attention to Puff. She came over and nestled on my lap, sort of nudging the kitten to the side.

"This is an adorable kitten," Mrs. Beasley told someone on the telephone. "But let's not offer her for adoption for about another two weeks. She's very small and will need some tender care before she's ready to go off into the world."

We went on two roundups the next week, one after school and one on Sunday. This time we went farther out into the woods near the edge of the turnpike. There were so many trees, I didn't think the cat lady would find anything out there. I followed behind her as she carried her trap, looking for the right place to set it down.

"This is a good area," she told me, pointing to a log that was stretched in front of a tiny brook.

"For some reason, maybe because there's water nearby, the stray cats settle around here." She seemed to know all their secret places. It was a race between Mrs. Beasley and her traps, and the traps some people set to catch the cats to destroy them. Or there were dogs out in the woods, or cars on the turnpike. So many dangers to the cats while they were wild. Mrs. Beasley never forgot that. She always worried about the cats who had no homes, and especially about the cats she'd saved that nobody wanted. She would have to set them free again when it got too crowded in her house. But Mrs. Beasley always tried to find a safe area to let her cats go, some place where they could hunt for their own food. And when the weather was bad, she would be sure to leave out dishes of store-bought food for them.

"You're spending an awful lot of time over there," my mother said one day while she was dressing Greta. "Doesn't Miss Beasley mind? I don't want you to get in her way."

"She likes me," I explained. I almost wanted to tell her the whole truth, that I didn't get in the way there like I did here at home. I always seemed to be talking too loud, waking up poor Greta, or running around the house too much when my mother wanted it to be quiet. "I help her take care of the cats," I said proudly.

"Well, young man," my mother said, hugging me real tight for a moment, which surprised me, since Greta was the only one I had seen her hugging lately. "I sure wish you would help out a little more around here. You didn't take out the garbage yesterday or today. And remember, the newspapers have to be tied in bunches because they've started recycling in the town. We have to tie them up and place them on the curb once a month."

"Sure." I nodded. "I'll do it."

"Not good enough, honey," my mother answered. "Please go down to the cellar and start making the piles now. The men come tomorrow for pickup, and I know you'll forget."

I went down to the cellar and put on the light. While I was piling up the papers I began to think what a perfect place the cellar would be for Grey. We could keep her kitty litter there and even her water and food if my parents didn't want her upstairs. It was warm in the cellar because of the heater. My mom had her washer and dryer down there, and some baskets with blankets in them. I could just see Grey snuggling up real cozy on a winter night, then maybe coming upstairs and sleeping with me when she felt like it, which would probably be all the time.

So when I went upstairs, I told my mom about my great idea. It was one of those times when I knew what her answer would be even as I asked, "Can I bring Grey home?"

My mother was holding Greta in one arm while mixing the spaghetti sauce. She put on a very thoughtful face. "Honey, I knew this would happen. That's why I was worried about you spending so much time over there. Frankie, I'm afraid to bring a cat into the house now with Greta so young. Bringing an animal into the house is like bringing another human being home to live with the family. It's not as easy as it looks."

Well, I sure agreed with her about that. Things had been terrific with just the three of us — me, Mom, and Dad. And I was sure Grey wouldn't cause half the trouble Greta did.

"I would take care of Grey," I said. "You wouldn't have to do anything."

"I just don't think this is a very good time for us or even for the pet. There's so much commotion around here now. Maybe next year, when Greta's a little older, we'll talk about it."

I couldn't imagine waiting a year to have Grey for my own. Besides, Mrs. Beasley would probably find a home for her before then. Anyone who had any sense would want Grey for a friend. In fact, I was surprised Mrs. Beasley hadn't found a family for her weeks ago.

# 4

Every day I thought about Grey being adopted by someone else. I'd listen to Mrs. Beasley call a few people, telling them about her cats — the new one we had found behind Michael's grocery store near the garbage cans, half frozen in the winter winds; the one we had found stuck beneath someone's porch with sticker bushes in his fur. In fact, I was beginning to wish Mrs. Beasley wouldn't pick up that telephone anymore when I went over.

That's all I thought about day after day. Grey and Mrs. Beasley's telephone. I thought about her adoption service and how one day I would show up at Mrs. Beasley's place and there would be one less grey cat there. Grey would be gone and the cat lady would tell me she had found a home for her. I thought about it when I was eating, and sometimes I would just push my food away because it didn't seem to matter that I ate it at all.

"What is it?" my mother asked, looking at me

with that worried frown. "Don't you feel well today, Frankie?"

"I'm okay," I said, thinking about Grey's soft fur and picturing Mrs. Beasley telling someone, "This is Grey. She'd make a wonderful pet in your home. She's so sweet and she never scratches or uses her claws. All she needs is love."

I just couldn't let that happen.

"How about working on this puzzle with me?" my dad asked one night. He had one of his five-hundred-piece puzzles laid out on the card table in the living room. We used to work on them all the time before Greta came along. Now in the evening he usually was busy helping my mother feed Greta, or dress her, or he was just playing with her. Even though he'd ask me to play, too, I felt Greta didn't really know the difference if I was there or not.

I missed working on the puzzles with my dad and was glad to have a chance to sit down at the table. I thought maybe he would have a different feeling about Grey because sometimes I could ask him permission to do something, and he would say yes when my mom said no. Then they would have this meeting, usually away from me, somewhere up in the bedroom or back in the kitchen. I decided to make one more try.

"Mrs. Beasley has this real special cat," I said. I told him about Grey, and her white nose, her big green eyes, and the little limp she had that wasn't serious — it was just from being thrown out into the street at night. I also told my dad how Grey would settle in my lap like a warm pillow.

"Here, put this orange piece over there." He took the puzzle from my hand. "That's part of the border." My dad was quiet for a moment, and I thought maybe he hadn't heard what I said. "Look, Frankie, I know things have been hard for you these past weeks, with your sister coming into the house. A new baby causes a lot of excitement and a lot of changes. You and I haven't had the time to spend together the way we used to, and I promise it's going to be different very soon. But I don't think the solution to all of this is a cat. Not now. Your mom would be very nervous with the cat running underfoot."

"But Grey isn't that kind of cat," I told my father. I didn't much care about the puzzle anymore. "Grey isn't like that. She isn't a wild cat. She doesn't run around breaking things. She just needs lots of love."

"I don't think the time is right." My dad's voice was getting stronger and one eyebrow rose the way it usually did when he was finished talking about something.

*   *   *

I didn't sleep all that night. I kept getting up and looking down the street toward Mrs. Beasley's house on the corner. I kept thinking about Grey sitting there and wondered if she was thinking about me over here. I kept thinking about Mrs. Beasley's telephone that kept ringing with people who wanted cats, and about The Friends of Cats, who were always looking for parents for the lost kittens. Grey was about four months old now. I knew, according to Mrs. Beasley's calendar, that something had to be done about Grey pretty soon or she would be too old for adoption. Most people like the younger pets. If she wasn't adopted soon, Mrs. Beasley would have to have her fixed, and then would come the big decision: when to return her to the environment where she had been found. Mrs. Beasley kept some cats way beyond the five months. They stayed because they had become her pets. But Grey wasn't like that — she was mostly mine.

The next day I had to ask Mrs. Beasley what would become of Grey.

"What about Grey?" she answered, picking her up and handing her to me the way she usually did when I arrived.

"I've been wondering why you haven't offered her for adoption."

"Do you want to adopt her?" she asked.

I hadn't expected that question. "Sure," I said.

"Wonderful." Mrs. Beasley's face brightened. "I knew the moment Grey sat on your lap she was your cat and no one else's. Do you want to take her home today?"

That question sent my stomach spinning. Grey had fallen asleep in my lap with her face up and her white nose pointed in the air. I knew at that moment I should have told the cat lady about Greta and my parents' decision, but the words just wouldn't come out. All I could feel was Grey's body close to mine. Just petting her made me feel good.

"I just have to wait a little while," I told the cat lady. "Another couple weeks until my sister gets a little older." I lied. It wasn't easy lying because I didn't do it often.

"Oh, that's just fine," the cat lady said. "Grey is a pleasure to have around."

"You won't offer her for adoption, will you?" I asked.

"You bet I won't," she answered.

"My mom loves cats, but I don't want to bother her this minute about Grey. You know — with Greta always needing something. I'd just as soon give her another week or two before I bring Grey home."

"That sounds very wise," Mrs. Beasley agreed

as she handed me a kitty litter pan to clean. I gently put Grey back on the ground.

"I don't want her to know anything about the cat until things settle down," I went on to tell Mrs. Beasley. I felt I could trust her with some of the truth, even though I didn't want to tell her that I wasn't at all sure when things would settle down.

"I guess a new baby can really cause a lot of excitement," Mrs. Beasley said. She handed me the bag of kitty litter. "But remember, Frankie, you don't want to wait too long. If you do, and then decide not to adopt Grey, you'll ruin her chances with someone else. By then she'll be quite big, and she does have that limp. People will notice that and it might hurt her chances for adoption if she becomes too old."

"I just need a little while longer." I kept lying because I couldn't give Grey up.

Mrs. Beasley looked very serious when she said, "I'm sorry if I'm getting cranky, young man. It's just that in the winter, it gets difficult to adopt out the kittens. As you can see, it's getting pretty crowded in here."

I looked around the living room and realized there were cats all over the place. There were cats on the steps coming down from her bedroom and I knew there were at least two cats in each room upstairs. Puff was a new addition to the family and Whitey wasn't going anywhere. She had been around for four years. Grey limped about the living room, and my heart just sort of flipped over when I thought about her going on the outside again, fending for herself.

Jimmy woke up just about then. He wiped his face with the bright red handkerchief he always kept in his pocket. "Anything more you want me to do?" he asked Mrs. Beasley.

"No, Jim, you did just fine. Go home and get some rest."

I didn't know why Jimmy had to say that. He did nothing but sleep in the rocking chair whenever I saw him, or eat some food Mrs. Beasley had set out on a plate for him. Jimmy would sometimes forget it was dinnertime unless she reminded him. I was beginning to think that Jimmy was part of Mrs. Beasley's family. I wondered what would happen to him if Mrs. Beasley ever left the neighborhood.

I went home angry that night, and I guess I stayed angry all week. It didn't seem fair what was happening to Mrs. Beasley, and it didn't seem fair what was happening to me.

I didn't finish tying the newspapers for the recycling truck, and when my parents asked me to take out the garbage, I waited until they asked three times, and then I got there just in time to see the garbage truck passing my house without our garbage. My parents weren't too happy about that.

I left my towels on the bathroom floor after I took a shower, even though I knew my mother would yell after me, "Frankie, throw your towels in the hamper." Well, to tell the truth, I didn't think the towels or the garbage or anything else going on in my house were as important as what was going to happen to Grey if I didn't do something quick.

I felt the same about school. I wasn't paying attention to what was going on. Denny and I didn't have much to talk about, either. He didn't want to talk about cats and I didn't want to talk about sports.

"Mrs. Simon called," my mother said after dinner one night. "She said you aren't turning in your homework and that you didn't finish your project on caterpillars."

I put on my worst face and answered, "Mrs. Simon is a crab."

That got me three days in my room after school. I couldn't go to the cat lady's house until the end of the three days and only if all my homework assignments were finished, including the report on caterpillars. I caught up with everything as quickly as I could. I never knew a clock could move so slowly as it did during the three days I couldn't visit Grey.

# 5

What happened, Frankie? Were you sick?"
Mrs. Beasley asked when she opened the
front door. There were two new cats sitting by
her feet, looking up at me.

"Just had some homework to catch up with," I
told her. "Is Grey here? Is she okay?"

"Yes, don't worry. She's here." Mrs. Beasley
patted my head as if I were one of her cats, but
her blue eyes weren't as bright as usual. Grey
hurried down the steps as if she had missed me.
Her voice was much louder than usual when she
meowed her hello.

"My, she missed you," the cat lady said.

Grey had kept a lot on her mind while I had
been away. She meowed under my chin, now and
then raising her head and looking straight into my
eyes. I bet she spoke to me that way for about
fifteen minutes. I think she told me I'd better not
stay away for so long again.

The doorbell rang and the cat lady answered it. It was Mrs. Baxter, the neighbor who lived two houses up from Mrs. Beasley.

"Your cats keep sitting on my window ledge," Mrs. Baxter complained. "Every morning when I wake up and open the shades, there they are, the two of them, a big brown cat and a black one with the meanest eyes."

"Oh, that's just Dusty and Fretful," Mrs. Beasley answered. "Fretful isn't mean. He's just a worrier. I guess that's because he was left to starve in the lot of the supermarket. Dusty and Fretful are rowdy boys. They insist on running out in the morning no matter how hard I try to keep them in. I really will try harder, I promise."

"I'm sorry, Mrs. Beasley. That's not good enough." Mrs. Baxter didn't look very comfortable standing there. "I've told you that I don't like the cats' paper plates. They blow all over my front yard. And there's always one cat or another running through my property. I'm going to a township meeting to complain this week. I'm sorry, Mrs. Beasley. Several of us cannot live with this situation."

"Oh, dear," Mrs. Beasley sighed, right after Mrs. Baxter marched down the street. "Whatever am I going to do?" She sat down on the couch, looking sadder then Fretful, who sat on the windowsill, looking after Mrs. Baxter as if he understood everything she had said.

Mrs. Beasley didn't talk much that whole afternoon. Jimmy came over and we cleaned up the house, dusting the furniture, scrubbing the floors. I knew if my mother saw me she would probably say, "Frankie, why can't I get you to do any of that at our house?" I didn't know why, except that Mrs. Beasley seemed to need my help and Grey needed my love. No one needed anything from me at home anymore except for me to take out the garbage and tie up the newspapers.

All week the news from Mrs. Beasley's house was not good. It was as if the cats knew something terrible was going to happen and they would be involved. They sat around just doing a lot of staring out of the windows, and at me, Mrs. Beasley, and Jimmy. Each day Mrs. Beasley told me something that upset my stomach. On Monday there was the township meeting. Everyone went there to complain about Mrs. Beasley.

"You couldn't imagine how they complained about my cats," Mrs. Beasley told me. "My goodness, Frankie. I sat there in the back of the room, listening, and I couldn't believe my ears. Poor Peanut Butter, who is afraid of his own shadow and never hurt a soul. One woman complained he was eating her flowers. And Sapphire, well that little cat just loves everyone. There was a man at the meeting who said Sapphire teased his big German shepherd. Can you imagine that? Sapphire loves dogs. She even cleaned the little puppy we had here for a week."

It was bad enough that no one had anything nice to say about Mrs. Beasley and her cats. But then the neighbors began to do mean things. Some people took away the paper plates Mrs. Beasley left on the steps for any stray cats who needed a meal. Others, the cat lady told me, were setting traps of their own to catch the cats and take them away to the animal shelters. "We have to be very careful about our family now," Mrs. Beasley told me. "I've been going around the neighborhood checking wherever I can to make sure there are no cats in the traps. It's taking up all my spare time."

And then there were the hoses. Some of the people in the neighborhood were hosing the cats whenever they would see them running on their lawns.

"Look at poor Sapphire this morning," Mrs. Beasley said, holding Sapphire's wet body in her arms. "It's just about freezing out there and someone sprayed him with water."

I was glad that Grey didn't like the outside and spent her days taking in the sun on one of Mrs. Beasley's window ledges. At least I didn't have to worry about her getting hurt.

I had so many things worrying me inside that I felt I was going to burst if I didn't tell someone. So I wrote to Grandpop Willie. I told him everything, and when I got to the end of the letter, I asked for his help. *Do you think, Grandpop Willie, that you could talk to Mom and Dad about Grey?*

I had just returned from mailing the letter when my mother called me into the kitchen. "Frankie, I saw Mrs. Beasley today — I was walking up with Greta to Main Street. This is the first time we've had a chance to talk."

I knew what was coming. I guess I knew it was coming ever since I had told Mrs. Beasley I could take Grey home in a few weeks. Those few weeks had passed, and though Mrs. Beasley didn't mention it to me again, I knew it was on her mind. Especially now that she had to worry about a home for most of the stray cats in her family.

"It seems you've given Mrs. Beasley the impression you're bringing Grey home to live with us."

"I didn't say right away," I answered, feeling my face grow hot the way it did when I was caught not telling the whole truth.

"Maybe not. But Mrs. Beasley had the idea that it's not going to be too long before Grey has a home. Frankie, this just isn't a good time for us to introduce a pet into the family. I thought we made that clear. I explained that to Mrs. Beasley."

I sat there with the words stuck in my throat. No one had asked me if it was a good time to introduce *Greta* into the family.

"When will it be a good time?" I asked.

"Maybe when Greta gets a little older." Mom ruffled my hair and kissed me on the cheek. "Don't worry. We'll get a cat some day."

I pulled away from my mother. "I don't want any cat. I want Grey," I yelled. My face felt stiff, the way it gets when I need a good cry. But I didn't want to cry now. I wanted to make my mother and father understand that this was an emergency situation and that every day Grey got a little older.

I didn't sleep all that night. I thought of the letter on the way to Grandpop Willie and figured it would take two days to get there. I knew Grandpop was the kind of person who liked to mind his own business. I hoped he would consider Grey his business as well as mine. I sat by the window just before the sun came up, watching the snow come down and wondering if Grey was sitting there by her window watching it also. Was she waiting for me, knowing in her heart she was mine and I was hers? Was she disappointed that I was taking so long to bring her home?

Everyone was still asleep when I finally went into Greta's room. I walked over to the crib and stared down at her. I couldn't believe anyone that small could take up so much space in one house. She was sucking her thumb, making all kinds of sounds. I stood there wondering just how long it would take her to grow bigger, to stop crying in the middle of the night, to stop needing so many diaper changes, to stop eating every couple of hours, to stop needing to be burped, held, played with. Were they talking about a year, or two years? Or maybe I'd be in high school before this house was ready for a pet. Greta kicked her feet in the air and smiled at me. I tried not to smile back but finally I gave her a little one before I walked out of the room.

I stayed away from Mrs. Beasley's house all week. I didn't want to know what was going on there. I didn't want to see the hurt in her eyes every time she found out someone else on the block wanted her to move. I didn't want to see her get all nervous each time Sapphire or Fretful managed to run out the front door when she wasn't looking. I didn't want to see the way she looked over at Jimmy with that worried look, as if she were wondering who would take care of him if she wasn't next door. But most of all I didn't want to know about Grey. Grey was six months old now and she would have to be fixed. And Mrs. Beasley knew she didn't have a home for her anymore.

# 6

Each day I took the long way around to school and back, making sure I didn't pass by Mrs. Beasley's house. I even went back to playing with Denny after school, though my mind wasn't on anything we did, even when we took our sleds during a thick snowstorm and slid down the hill near the school. It was one of those perfect sledding snowstorms, but somehow it didn't take away the emptiness I felt inside.

Grandpop Willie's letter didn't help, either.

*"Dear Willie,*

*Well, son, I tried. Let me tell you, I know what it's like to want a pet and not have one. Grandmom loves this condominium but as for me, well, when our old dog Benny died, nothing seemed exactly the same. I keep thinking we should get another dog, but Grandmom says they're a lot of trouble to take care of. All I know is that I never had a better friend than Bennie. One good friend like him is worth a million dollars. But that doesn't solve your problem, does it? Son, I tried. I called your mom and reminded her of the pets she had when she was a little girl. Of course, we had outdoor cats then. Most were strays from around the neighborhood that we fed and took care of. One finally came inside and made its home at the end of your mother's bed. But reminding her of all that didn't do the job. I think she's just a bit over-tired now, what with the new baby, and she isn't in the mood to give out too much un-derstanding about anything. She says just be patient, she doesn't mean you can't have a pet ever. It's just for a while. I'm sorry, buddy. I tried.*

I guess after Grandpop's letter, I might have stayed away forever from the cat lady's house because I felt it would break my heart to go there and not see Grey's face. I was sure she had been given away by this time. Anyone would want a cat like Grey.

Then I saw the sign one day. You could see it even from my front porch. FOR SALE. It was white with big black lettering. Mrs. Beasley was selling her house.

I could not get that sign out of my head all

morning. First thing, on my way home from school, I walked up the driveway with the paper plates like a small trail leading to Mrs. Beasley's front door. I rang the doorbell and waited, my heart jumping all over the place in my chest. I felt my eyes mist over and hoped some day Greta would realize what she had cost me. I would tell her. I would remember every little minute of the hurt I felt losing Grey, and I would tell her I hoped she never got a cat, either.

"Well, for goodness' sakes, Frankie. Where have you been? I thought perhaps you had become ill. You know there is this awful flu around. I was going to call you in a day or two if you didn't show up."

"No, I'm okay," I answered, looking around the living room. There were some new faces on the sofa and on the red chair, and there was a very small kitten in the kitten training box. Jimmy looked as if he hadn't moved, his chin resting on his chest as he slept in the rocking chair.

I didn't ask about Grey. I didn't think I could without crying, and I wasn't about to do that in front of Mrs. Beasley. She had enough troubles on her mind.

"You're selling your house?" I asked.

"Yes, I am, Frankie. The people around here just don't understand what I'm doing. They say the cats are the problem. Truthfully, I think the people are the problem. They're the ones hurting the cats, abandoning them, not feeding them, turning them away when they get old. They are not treating them with respect, like family. If they did, I wouldn't have any cats here."

"But where are you going to go?" I asked. "I mean, you just can't pick up and move all of them, can you?"

"I can do anything I want," Mrs. Beasley answered, her lips tightening up the way mine did when I was getting ready to take a difficult shot in basketball.

"Where's Tabby?" I asked, afraid to ask about Grey. The red-and-orange cat was missing.

"Gave him a nice home yesterday," Mrs. Beasley said. "Want to see the two new kittens in isolation?"

I didn't want to see any cat but Grey, but I followed her up the long winding stairway. "Don't you miss Tabby?" I asked. "He was here for so long." I was thinking about Grey when I said that, wondering how I would get used to not seeing her again. I was certain Mrs. Beasley had placed Grey back in her environment.

"You have to remember, Frankie. This is a holding place. All the cats pass through here, but my purpose always is to find them a good and loving home. To match a family with a cat."

We went upstairs into the isolation room. It was

also called The Get Well Room. Two little kittens no bigger than my hand were running about the room. A large black cat lay in the corner watching them and us. The kittens ran over my feet when they saw me.

"There's someone else you might want to say hello to," Mrs. Beasley said as we left the room. She opened up the door to the other Get Well Room. There, on the radiator, was Grey, all puffed up in a ball.

"I had to lock her up yesterday and today. I took her to the veterinarian to have her fixed. She's six months old and I didn't want to wait any longer. She's been taking it easy, recuperating."

I scooped up Grey in my arms. If I was afraid for a minute she had forgotten me, she wiped those fears away real fast. She began to lick my chin, my cheeks. She even stretched up to reach my eyes. I kept them closed, laughing as she washed my face with her rough tongue.

"Whether you take Grey or not," Mrs. Beasley said, "she's your cat. We can't place her anywhere else. That wouldn't be fair to you or to her. But don't worry, Frankie. Time is on our side. You'll see. Greta will grow. I spoke to your mother. She's a very sweet lady. One day she'll wake up and realize that Grey is just what she needs to settle her house down."

That's all she said about the matter, but I wasn't

about to question her. Mrs. Beasley had a way of knowing about things, and she didn't like to give away the answers all at once.

The doorbell rang and we hurried downstairs. A lady stood there with a small child. He looked to be about three years old and he was walking sort of wobbly.

"Can I help you?" Mrs. Beasley asked.

"Yes, I'd like Barry to pick out a kitten."

"Barry?" Mrs. Beasley asked.

"My son." She picked up the child. "Barry needs a playmate. We heard you have many kittens. We'd like a small one so that it doesn't get too rough with him."

Barry grabbed hold of the tail of one of the smaller cats and began pulling it as if he were holding a rope. Mrs. Beasley's face screwed up in a knot, the way it did when she got angry. The color left her cheeks.

"I really don't have any kittens right now," she said.

"But what about the kitten in the cage?" The woman pointed to the playful kitten rolling around in the kitty litter.

"She's not for adoption," Mrs. Beasley said.

I knew Mrs. Beasley wanted to get rid of as many cats as she could, especially now that she had to move, so I didn't understand what the problem was until after the woman left.

"She just wants a kitten as a toy for that little boy, something that he can twirl around by the tail. She didn't even scold him for the way he was treating the cat. That told me a lot. I do not let my cats go to homes where the people have no manners."

She handed me a comb and we groomed the cats. Grey, of course, got my attention first, and later she stayed right by my foot.

Then we went on a roundup and left some cages stacked with food in the woods, behind some shopping center parking lots, and in back of Mr. Matt's grocery store.

It felt so good to see Grey again, but something was missing now when I went to Mrs. Beasley's house. I always had to pass that FOR SALE sign and it reminded me that one day Mrs. Beasley and her cats wouldn't be down the block anymore. And neither would Grey. I didn't know what I would do when that happened and I guess Mrs. Beasley didn't either because she never talked about the sign or the house sale. In fact, she was going on as if nothing different were happening around her, except she was very careful about the cats running loose.

I was also trying to be very careful at home. I got the idea that if I paid attention to my homework and did all my chores and even some that weren't mine, maybe my parents would reward me. Maybe they would think a great reward would be giving me Grey. So I was very busy during the month of March.

Greta was busy, too. She was trying to eat some sloppy-looking baby food by herself and kept managing to push her spoon all over her face. By the time the meals were over, there was food on the floor, on her clothes, and sometimes even on me when it splattered about. Everyone at the table thought it was funny. I didn't think they would find it so funny if I was doing it.

"You're always so busy lately," my dad said to me one night after I had turned on the television set. "It seems you and I don't have any time together."

We sat on the sofa next to one another. I couldn't really think of anything to say. We had gotten out of the habit of talking to each other. I didn't think Dad would be interested in anything I had to say anyway, because all I wanted to do was talk about Grey.

"How's school?" my dad asked.

"Okay," I answered.

"Need any help with your homework?"

"Not really," I answered.

"How's Denny?"

"I don't see him that much anymore," I said. It didn't seem that we had much to talk about lately; Denny wasn't interested in Mrs. Beasley's problems. If I said to him, "I hope a SOLD sign isn't in front of Mrs. Beasley's house today," Denny would just look at me as if I had said something stupid.

After a while, my dad gave up talking to me. We just sat on the couch, watching television. I wondered if he had as many things buzzing around inside his head as I did. Once, when there was a commercial break, I walked over to the living room window and looked out. I needed to know if the FOR SALE sign was still up in front of the cat lady's house. I couldn't see it, though, and finally sat down.

"What were you looking at?" my dad asked.

"Nothing special," I answered. I didn't think it would help to tell him the truth.

# 7

During the spring break, we went to my grandparents' condominium for a little vacation. Dad took off from work for a couple of days and Mom packed up Greta with her playpen and diapers and all the things she needed to get by. Half the car belonged to Greta.

My grandparents had a guest room for my parents and Greta, and a pull-out couch for me in the living room. I usually liked to go there because Grandpop Willie would take me to the arcade and we'd play the pinball machines all day. Dad would only go for an hour or so and then he'd get restless, but Grandpop Willie had all the time in the world and he never rushed me about going home.

"I won't be back for a whole week," I told Mrs. Beasley before I left. I gave Grey a real long hug and tried to explain to her that a week wasn't a very long time.

"Don't worry," Mrs. Beasley said. "We'll be here when you get back. Even when a house is sold, it takes weeks, sometimes months, for the contracts to be signed. So don't worry, Frankie. Go and have some fun."

It was easy to have fun with Grandpop Willie. He and Grandmom lived near the ocean and we spent the first two days off by ourselves, walking on the beach, even though it was cold and not too many people were there with us.

"You're awfully quiet, young man," Grandpop Willie said to me while we picked up seashells. "You haven't said much since you got here."

I shrugged my shoulders and hoped he understood what I was thinking. Grandpop didn't disappoint me.

"Grey's still got hold of you, hasn't she? Your parents are worried about you, Frankie. They say you don't have the pep you used to have. They think maybe it's because Greta's around. They realize they haven't been paying that much attention to you. But I don't think it's Greta that's got you down as much as it is Grey."

As usual, Grandpop Willie had hit the nail right on the head.

"But it's Greta's fault anyway," I said. "If she wasn't around I could get Grey."

"If she wasn't around, maybe you wouldn't want Grey," Grandpop Willie answered. "But that doesn't cure the problem, does it?" Grandpop Willie and I were sitting on the boardwalk with our feet up against the railings. The salt air had the smell of fish to it.

"That's the nice thing about living down here," Grandpop said. "You can come up to the boardwalk and dump all your problems into the ocean. Then you can go home without them."

"The ocean isn't going to help me," I answered. "While I'm here, Mrs. Beasley might be selling her house. I won't even know it."

"Then how about if we go back to the apartment and you make a call to her. Just find out how Grey is and what's going on."

"Thanks, Gramps," I said, wrapping my arms around his neck. He hadn't shaved that morning and his cheeks were rough, but it didn't matter. I felt his arms squeeze about me and I knew that between us we'd find a way to bring Grey home.

When we got back to the condominium, I dialed Mrs. Beasley's number and waited. It usually took her about three rings to answer the telephone because she had a flight of steps to come down and lots of cats to run around. It rang three times, then four, then five, but no one answered.

I must have run over to use the telephone about ten times that night. No one answered then or even the next morning. Mrs. Beasley never went out like that and left the cats for so long. They had to be fed and their water needed changing. I couldn't imagine where she was or why she didn't answer the telephone.

There was nothing I wanted to do after that. I didn't even want to go to the arcade with Grandpop. "Maybe she left someone in charge to take care of the cats." Grandpop Willie tried to make me feel better when I told him how worried I was. "Maybe something came up in her family and she had to go away for a couple of days."

"She has no family but the cats, and Jimmy is the only one who helps her. He couldn't do it without Mrs. Beasley telling him what to do. Something's wrong. I know it." If I could have, I would have left for home right then.

I lost my appetite. Grandmom Sarah made those special desserts that I always cleaned off her big flowered plates, but this time I just sat there staring at them.

My mom took my temperature because she thought I had a virus. My dad sat me on his lap and tried to find out what was going on. But I couldn't tell him that I thought Mrs. Beasley was in trouble and so were the cats and I wanted to go home right then and see what happened. So I waited and waited, watching the clock tick so slowly I thought it was just teasing me. I kept trying to call Mrs. Beasley when no one was around except Grandpop. Finally it was time to pack up our suitcases and go home.

I was the first one packed and by the front door. "Well," said Grandmom Sarah, "you certainly didn't enjoy yourself this visit." She looked cross and I knew she was hurt because I didn't appreciate any of her cooking. "I certainly hope Grandpop Willie knows what he's doing, going home with you now when you're in such a bad mood."

That came as a real surprise. Grandpop came to the front door with his suitcase packed. He had one of those broad grins on his face. "You won't mind if we spend a few days together just hanging out, will you, Frankie?" he asked. He grabbed my hand and squeezed it, as if there were a secret message delivered between the two of us.

My heart just about dropped into my shoes when we passed the FOR SALE sign in front of Mrs. Beasley's house. The whole house was dark. Mrs. Beasley always left a light on in an upstairs room and one in the living room downstairs. But there wasn't a single light on in the house.

"Fearful is afraid of the dark," I told Grandpop.

"Mrs. Beasley always leaves a light on for him and the other cats."

"You want to go over and check things out?" Grandpop asked. It was dark and past my bedtime. I doubted if my parents would allow that. I told Grandpop what I thought.

"You let me handle it," he said. We went downstairs into the living room, where my mother was sorting through the suitcases.

"I don't think there's a clean piece of clothing in here," she said. She wasn't in a very good mood, but that didn't stop Grandpop.

"I need to stretch my legs," he said. "Is it okay for Frankie to walk with me? You know I'm not so familiar with this neighborhood."

"Sure, Dad," my mom answered. "Just don't be too long. Frankie has school tomorrow."

"You're great," I said to Grandpop as we rushed down the block toward the cat lady's house. I knew something was wrong the minute we reached Mrs. Beasley's porch. The curtains in all of the windows were closed and there wasn't one cat sitting in the window.

I knocked on the door and waited. Fearful didn't pop up from behind the curtain the way he usually did. Neither did Grey. I went around to every window on the bottom floor but not one cat appeared. I called Pee Wee's name into some of the bushes in the backyard. I waited. There wasn't even a rustle. "Brilliant. Jo Jo." Then I guess I got really excited and began knocking a little hard on the front door, shouting Grey's name.

Jimmy must have heard me next door because he opened his bedroom window and sleepily rubbed his eyes. "What's doin', Frankie?"

"Where is Mrs. Beasley?" I asked.

"Mrs. Beasley . . ." Jimmy hung over the window thinking for minute. "She's in the hospital," he said. "Sick. Took her in yesterday. "No," he shook his head. "Maybe it was a couple of days ago."

"Where are the cats?" I asked, my throat dry, the words sort of clinging to the roof of my mouth.

Jimmy scratched his head. It was as if I were giving him a test and he wasn't sure about the answers to the questions. I could tell he was trying to remember.

"Grey. Fearful." I tried to help his memory. "You know, the cats you help her with."

"I know," Jimmy finally answered. "They're at the animal shelter."

"No," I called up to his window. "Mrs. Beasley would never send the cats away like that." I was hoping he had made a big mistake but he kept shaking his head.

"Yup. They came in a wagon and rounded them up," he answered. Then he pulled down the window and disappeared back into his bedroom.

"I guess they thought Jimmy wouldn't be able to take care of all the cats by himself," I told Grandpop Willie.

Grandpop's hand pressed my shoulder. Then I felt his arms around me. It was dark enough that I knew he wouldn't see my tears, so I let them go as he held me.

# 8

I didn't go to school the next day. I just lay in my bed when my alarm clock went off.

"I knew you were coming down with something," my mother said when she saw me lying there. "You look so pale." She put her hand on my forehead. "You don't seem to have a fever. Does your stomach feel upset? I knew you weren't yourself when you didn't eat the chocolate cupcakes Grandmom made for you. Maybe I should call Doctor Benson."

I spent part of the morning sitting in Doctor Benson's office. After the examination, he said, "Frankie looks okay to me, Mrs. Hayes. Keep an eye on him today. He should be well enough to go to school tomorrow if there are no new symptoms."

"Try to rest," my mother said when we got home. "I don't think you've been getting enough sleep lately."

I was tired because I don't think I closed my

eyes the night before. But when I got upstairs, I couldn't lie down. I just kept staring out the window across the street and down the block. I kept hoping Jimmy was wrong. I kept wishing Mrs. Beasley's old beat-up station wagon would start up. I usually could see the exhaust coming out from its tailpipe or hear it making a loud clanking noise whenever the cat lady started it in cold weather.

When my mom gave me some hot tea and a comic book she had bought me, she said, "Did you hear about Mrs. Beasley? She had her gall bladder out. She'll be laid up for quite a while, poor thing." My mother put her hand on my forehead again. Then she set down a plate of saltine crackers with jam on the nightstand next to my bed. She put the portable television on in my room. "It won't be too bad, watching your favorite programs, will it?" She was smiling as she put away some clean clothes into my bureau.

"Where's Grandpop Willie?" I asked.

"He went down to the park to feed the birds."

I waited until my mom went out of the room. There was no time to read or to watch television. Mrs. Beasley was in trouble and she needed me. I looked at the clock on the nightstand. It was about 11:30, time for Greta's nap. Usually my mom did her wash in the laundry room while my sister was sleeping. I could almost hear Mrs.

Beasley's voice, as if she were standing in the room with me. "I wouldn't know what to do without my cats," she said. "They wouldn't know what to do without me, either."

I knew I had to do something or we would lose all the cats, and Grey would be lost to me forever. I put on my trousers and jersey, snuck down the steps to the living room, and grabbed my jacket from the coat closet. I looked around. It was quiet in the house. Then I heard my mom singing downstairs in the laundry room. Carefully, I opened the front door and ran down the street toward the park.

I found Grandpop Willie sitting on a bench with birds flying all around him. He was scattering the birdseed at his feet.

"Hi, there," he called when he saw me. "I thought maybe you wanted to take a nap this morning. You didn't get much sleep last night."

"I'm sorry I kept you up," I answered, sitting down on the bench next to him. The best part of Grandpop Willie's visit was that we always shared the bunk beds in my bedroom. Grandpop loved to sleep on top.

"I didn't sleep that well, either, son. In fact, I've been sitting here all morning trying to think of a way out of this thing. There has to be something we can do to help Mrs. Beasley."

I guess it was because I was so tired, or maybe

because I felt sad, or maybe just because even sitting there with Grandpop Willie I felt so lonely without Grey. I didn't intend for it to happen, but I buried my head in Grandpop's shoulder and even though it was daylight, the saltwater ran from my eyes. I could taste it on my lips. It was embarrassing, but I just couldn't stop crying. I pictured Mrs. Beasley in the hospital and the cats, her friends, my Grey, locked up somewhere in cages at the shelter, or worse. What if they had been destroyed? I knew that the animal shelter couldn't keep stray pets forever.

"There, there, Frankie." Grandpop rubbed my head with his strong hands. I felt myself calm down. "Go ahead. Let it out. Get it all out of your system. It's good to cry, you know. I do it all the time."

"What do you cry about?" I asked, wiping my face with the handkerchief he handed me.

"Oh, lots of things. Sometimes I cry because I can't run as fast as I did when I was your age. Gosh, I miss running like that. Sometimes I cry when I can't read a name in the telephone book because the print is too small. Sometimes I just cry because I'm happy, like when I'm with you and I think I'm the luckiest guy alive to have such a fine grandson."

I felt very important when he told me that. I looked up into his face and sure enough, Grandpop had teardrops coming down from his clear blue eyes. He didn't seem ashamed about it. He just took the white handkerchief from my hands and wiped his face.

For a moment, sitting there in the park, there was no Greta, no school, no anything but the two of us sharing something special. But finally, I knew we had to get to work. Grandpop knew it, too.

"We can't just sit here, can we, Frankie? Something's got to be done about your friend and her family."

We went home to our house. Grandpop told my mother he and I had an errand to do and he would need her car.

"But Frankie's supposed to be in bed," she said.

"He's feeling just fine now, aren't you, Frankie?" Grandpop nudged me and I got the message.

I put on a bright smile. "All of a sudden, I feel my old self again," I said. Just to prove it, I went over to the fruit bowl on the table in front of the living room couch and picked up a banana and an apple. "I'll eat these on the way," I said.

"Okay." My mom looked at us as if she knew something was going on. "But make sure tomorrow you get up ready to go to school, Frankie."

We got into Mom's car. "Where are we going?" I asked.

"To the animal shelter," Grandpop answered. He stopped at a gas station, filled up the tank with gas, and asked directions.

The gas station attendant told us it was on Elm Street.

"What if they're not there?" I kept saying over and over as we parked the car and walked up the long driveway toward the shelter. I could hear the dogs yelping and barking. "What if they're all gone?"

"Think positively, young man," Grandpop Willie said. He was holding onto my hand as we walked. "They'll be there. Don't worry about it."

Grandpop walked up to the lady at the reception desk. "I wonder if you could please give me some information?" he asked.

"Certainly," she answered, smiling. "How can I help you?"

"I have a friend named Mrs. Beasley," Grandpop said. "Her cats are supposed to be here. I wondered what happened to them."

"Oh, yes, the 'Beasley Kids.' That's what Mrs. Beasley called them when she phoned from the hospital. She was so worried about her cats."

The woman looked through a bunch of cards in a box on her desk. It must have taken only a minute, but it felt like an hour to me. Then she looked up at Grandpop. "We promised to keep them one week for her. You know, it's such an unusual case, having all those cats come in at once. But Mrs. Beasley is special, the way she has taken care of them."

"When's the week up?" Grandpop asked.

"Actually, this afternoon," the woman answered, looking at the card again..

"Then what?" Grandpop asked.

"Then we offer them for adoption. She insisted that none be given away until she got out of the hospital. She likes to interview all the prospective families herself." The woman's eyes grew sad as she said, "But I don't think she's going to be out in time. I called this morning and they said she might have to stay in the hospital another week. She's healing slowly."

"But if they don't get adopted?" Grandpop asked.

The woman shrugged as if she didn't feel terrific about answering that question. "We just don't have the room to keep all of the animals forever," she answered, and we both knew what that meant. They would have to be destroyed. "We just don't have the money for their food and care. Of course, if more people would donate money, maybe we could keep more pets longer."

"Well, then, we'll just have to take them off your hands, won't we, Frankie?" Grandpop Willie pulled me over to the side, where the lady at the desk couldn't hear. He whispered, "Do you know any way we can get into Mrs. Beasley's house?"

I remembered my conversation with Mrs. Beasley one day when her car broke down and she got home late to feed her cats. She'd said, "If I ever need you to feed them for me, the key to the house is inside the hole in the tree in the backyard." I told Grandpop Willie.

Grandpop returned to the lady at the desk. "I'd like to adopt all of Mrs. Beasley's cats," he said.

"All of them?" the woman asked, her eyes opening wide.

"All of them," my grandpop repeated. "What time are they up for adoption?"

"Three o'clock this afternoon," she said. "Don't you want to see them before you adopt them?"

"Nope," Grandpop said. "We have too much to do to waste any time. Don't let any of them go until I get back. We have to get some cat carriers ready."

We left the shelter in a hurry. "We've got a lot of work to do, son. Let's get over to Mrs. Beasley's house and get things ready. You'll have to show me what she does."

We found the key where the cat lady usually left it. I opened the door. Everything was just the way I remembered it. The cage for the new little kittens was there. The empty food dishes were set on the floor just as if Mrs. Beasley expected all her cats for supper. The only thing different was that Mrs. Beasley and her cats were gone and the house had an empty feeling to it. We found three cat carriers in the basement.

Then we called Mrs. Beasley at the hospital. I told her about Grandpop Willie and what he was going to do and then I put him on the telephone.

"I'm going to stay around for a while and help Frankie take care of the cats," he told her. "So don't you worry about a thing."

When he got off the telephone, he told me, "Mrs. Beasley is going to call the shelter and tell them it's okay with her that we take her cats home. She's also going to tell them this isn't a regular adoption so we don't have to pay a fee for each cat."

"What's going on?" Jimmy asked as he walked into the kitchen. "I saw your car in the driveway."

"We're bringing Mrs. Beasley's cats home," I told him. "We're going to take care of them until she's better."

"Well, I sure can help with that," Jimmy said. "Why don't you go pick them up and I'll get all the food ready just the way I do for Mrs. Beasley." Jimmy sat down in his favorite rocking chair and patted the sides as if he had missed it.

"Come on, Frankie," said Grandpop. "We've got some trips to make."

The lady at the animal shelter got up from her seat as soon as she saw us coming down the hallway.

"We'll take three at a time," Grandpop said.

"There are about fifteen, you know," the lady said.

"That's fine with us," Grandpop answered. "It'll take us a while but we'll take them all."

# 9

Grey looked up at me as soon as I came into the room where all the cages were lined up. She was in a big cage with all of Mrs. Beasley's cats and she looked so sad, my heart just about broke when I saw her. Her fur was matted.

"Grey," I called into the cage, wanting to take every cat there home with me on the first trip. "We're going home." I took her gently in my arms and placed her in the carrier. Fearful and Princess were next. Fearful was meowing something terrible, as if she were complaining about the entire experience. Princess didn't look like a princess. Her white hair was matted as if no one had combed her.

We got them settled at home with Jimmy, who gave each cat a big hug and a welcome bowl of fresh food and water. He had Princess's favorite pink blanket laid out on the floor.

Fearful soon filled up her corner with her

brown-and-red body. Grey wouldn't go anywhere but next to me, rubbing against my leg, following me from one room to the other.

"I'll be right back," I told her. "We've got to bring home the others."

Grandpop and I worked hard the rest of the afternoon. I knew I could not have done it without him. It took us about fifteen minutes for the trip back and forth to the shelter and we had to make about four trips. Toward the end, we were able to put a few kittens into one carrier and Jo Jo, the Persian who never went anywhere, just sat in the backseat next to the filled carriers.

"Well, we really have our hands full," Grandpop said, while we were standing in the middle of about two dozen cats at the cat lady's house. Grandpop Willie had taken seven more from the shelter that he fell in love with, two of which he intended to take back with him to his condominium on Blueberry Road.

I almost hated to tell him we weren't finished yet. We had to go on a roundup. I knew there were certain spots where Mrs. Beasley had left traps. If there were cats caught in them, they could starve to death. Grandpop Willie and I left Jimmy napping in the rocking chair. We visited every stop on Mrs. Beasley's route. We only found three cages. They were empty.

That night when we finally got into bed, after Grandpop had listened to a long lecture from my mom on keeping me out all day and not calling in to let her know where we were, Grandpop leaned down from his top bunk bed. "We'll set up a schedule tomorrow. I'll take care of the morning shift while you're at school. We'll work it out."

"Don't forget to brush them and comb them," I told him sleepily. "They all have to get their dignity back."

I never had such a busy week. I tried very hard to keep my room clean, pick up my dirty clothes, and take out the garbage, so that my mother would understand when I went to Mrs. Beasley's house to take care of her chores. "You see, Frankie, if you do what has to be done at home and in school, then you're free to do what you have to do for Mrs. Beasley," Grandpop told me.

We thought Mrs. Beasley would be out by the end of the week, but the doctor decided to keep her another few days. "You don't know how good I feel knowing you're taking care of the cats," she told us over the telephone. "Frankie, I don't think I would have wanted to get well if I had lost my cats."

"I can't wait until Mrs. Beasley gets better," my mom said to my dad at the dinner table that night, but I had the feeling she was talking to Grandpop and me. Greta was propped up in her high chair. "Things just haven't been the same around here all week."

"Well, Jeanie, I must tell you I've been having a ball," Grandpop said. "I didn't realize how much I loved cats."

That was absolutely the wrong thing to say at our dinner table. "Well, I don't love them," my mom said, looking directly at Grandpop. "And I hope you both realize none of those cats are going to wind up here."

The mashed potatoes got stiff in my mouth. Grandpop Willie and I looked at one another as if we were both thinking the same thing. We were going to have to change Mom's mind.

Grandpop began right away. He started talking about the good old days when Mom had her own pet cat, Samantha, and how one day Samantha even followed her to school. Mom smiled when he repeated the story. He even reminded her of how Samantha took care of her when she was sick, sleeping by her side as if she were her nurse.

"I was just a little girl back then," my mom said.

"You'll never stop being a little girl to me," Grandpop told her as he took her in his arms.

Mrs. Beasley came home on Saturday at noon. She looked very thin and pale. A nurse came in and helped her walk very slowly up the steps. "I'll be taking care of her for a while," she said.

The cats welcomed Mrs. Beasley home. They followed her up the stairs, and as soon as she was settled in her bed, they jumped on it, taking positions by her feet, by her side, sitting there looking at her as if they understood she couldn't take too much excitement. While Grandpop Willie and I were downstairs cleaning out the litter boxes, I heard Mrs. Beasley giggle and I knew she was on her way to getting well.

"We've got a problem," Grandpop Willie said that evening after having a visit with Mrs. Beasley in her bedroom. "Mrs. Beasley is running out of money for cat food. She had a spot on cable television, a small five-minute section coming up on Monday, when she was supposed to bring one of her cats and talk about her adoption service. If she can't make it, she's afraid there won't be a way to interest the public in contributing money for all of this."

"What's she going to do?" I asked. "That's only two days away."

"She's a stubborn woman, she is. She says she's going to go on television if she has to be carried to the studio. Personally, I don't think she'll be strong enough."

We sat for a while on Mrs. Beasley's green couch, thinking about the problem. I held Grey in my lap, stroking her. That always made me feel better.

"We'll go for her," Grandpop Willie finally said. "We'll take Grey and that small orange kitten we just got. We know enough about Mrs. Beasley's family and how she takes care of them. We'll just tell everyone who's watching us."

Grandpop Willie marched back up the steps, and in a little while I heard Mrs. Beasley's voice, much stronger than it had been a few hours before, shout, "Oh, how wonderful of you!"

My mom and dad didn't think it was so wonderful when we told them the next day. "It means Frankie taking off from school again," my dad said when we told him. "Frankie, you told me you have a big test to study for. Aren't you taking it tomorrow?"

"He can make up a test," Grandpop Willie said.

"Dad, please don't interfere," my mom warned him. "These cats are monopolizing our lives. I really think Frankie has become too involved with them and with Mrs. Beasley. Besides, weren't you supposed to meet Mother tomorrow at Marilyn's house?"

Marilyn was my mother's sister and Grandmom Sarah had gone there to visit. "I was supposed to," Grandpop Willie said. "But I'm staying for a few days longer. Until Mrs. Beasley gets on her feet. Unless my daughter throws me out."

I felt this was getting to be an argument between my mother and Gramps and I wasn't sure who was going to win.

"Dad, don't be silly." My mom's face got real red. "You know you're welcome here for as long as you want to stay."

"Good," Grandpop answered. "Then stop making such a fuss about nothing. I already called the television station and told them we're coming, Frankie and me. They loved the fact there would be a young boy coming with a cat. We've decided to bring Grey."

There wasn't another word said about it the rest of the night. To tell you the truth, I wasn't so certain about this television appearance anymore. Mrs. Beasley said all I had to do was tell everyone about Grey and how I loved her, and Grandpop would talk about the money situation. But all night, while I lay in bed, I kept thinking that there would be a lot of people staring at my face tomorrow.

# 10

The next day, Mom took out the suit I usually wear on the holidays and a white shirt and tie from the closet. She brushed back my hair. "I wish you could have gotten a haircut," she said, smiling. "You look very handsome today." She kissed me on the cheek. "I'm still not too happy about your missing that test, but I guess it's for a good cause."

"This is just as much of a test as the one in school," Grandpop Willie said as he plunked his bright blue hat with the feather on his head. "Frankie is going on television to help someone. You couldn't learn anything more important than that."

"Okay, Dad," Mom said. "I get your point."

My dad helped me on with my coat. He hugged me before I left. "We're going to tune you in this morning, Frankie. In fact, I heard your mother calling just about everyone on the block."

Grey was already in the cat carrier with the

kitten when we got to Mrs. Beasley's. Jimmy had brushed her extra special and her fur was glistening. Her green eyes were bright and she meowed as soon as she saw me. Mrs. Beasley squeezed both my hands. She was sitting downstairs on the couch. "You look wonderful," she said to me. "I am so proud to have you represent Mrs. Beasley's Adoption Agency."

I wasn't prepared for the excitement when I got to the television station. There were cameras, three of them, pointing at Grey and me when we finally were seated in a chair opposite a lady with dark makeup around her eyes. The lights were hot and I began to perspire. Grey liked the heat. I think it reminded her of the sunbeam she usually rested beneath when she sat on Mrs. Beasley's windowsill.

"Your name is Frankie Hayes?" The lady wrote it down in her notebook when I said yes.

"Have you ever been on television before?" she asked.

I told her no.

"Well, just remember to look at me and try to forget the cameras around you. Think of this as just being in your living room at home, the two of us, and we're having a nice chat about cats."

I didn't think that was possible with the cameras zooming in on me, but when Grandpop Willie sat down next to me with the kitten I felt better about everything. He put his hand on mine. "We're going to do just fine," he said.

"Two minutes," a cameraman called out.

"I'll introduce you," the woman said, "and then I'll say, 'What would you like to say, Frankie, about Mrs. Beasley's cats?' When I ask you that, it's your turn to speak."

"One minute," the man behind the camera called.

I listened as the lady everyone called Barbara told the people watching at home about Mrs. Beasley's Adoption Agency and her need to raise funds. Then she petted Grey and asked me what I would like to say about Mrs. Beasley's cats.

Grey was purring in my lap, and now and then she licked my hand. She made it easy for me to talk about loving cats. "I guess I think everybody should have a cat," I said. "At least if it's a cat like Grey." I stroked Grey and she looked up at me for a minute before she stretched, then put her paws on my shoulders and washed my face. Barbara and Grandpop Willie laughed.

"Go on, Frankie," Barbara said. "Tell us some more about Grey."

"She's my best friend. I mean I have friends, good friends, but Grey never lets me down, never hurts me. She's the best listener and she's always there, never too busy to sit on my lap or wash my face, or sleep by my feet. I guess the best part is I'm never lonely when Grey's around. Whenever I'm with her, I don't have to worry about calling someone up to play or thinking why they didn't call me. It doesn't matter when Grey's around." By this time Grey was putting on some act, as if she knew she had hundreds, maybe thousands, of people watching her. She was sitting on my shoulder with her chin resting on my head, staring at Barbara as if she were listening and waiting to be interviewed herself.

"Is Grey your cat?" Barbara asked me.

"Yes, she is," I answered. "I mean, she doesn't live with me at my house, but Mrs. Beasley said she's my cat. She says Grey could never belong to anyone else because she loves me so much."

Then it was Grandpop Willie's turn to speak. He told everyone about Mrs. Beasley's Adoption Agency, about The Friends of Cats, about her roundups, about all the cats she had saved, about how she took such good care of her family. Barbara gave out a post office box address for contributions.

Grandpop Willie grabbed me in his arms when I was finished. "You did great, son. You did just great."

Everyone else at the television station must have agreed because they were petting Grey and hugging me. Grandpop Willie took Grey and me out for hamburgers and french fries at the drive-in. Grey had her own hamburger without the roll. Then we went home with Grey.

"It's about time your parents meet Grey in person," Grandpop said.

Mom and Dad were waiting for us in the living room. You would have thought I was someone special when I walked in. Mom was all smiles, and she stood up and walked right over to me. "Frankie," she said. "I can't believe how well you handled yourself on television. I was so proud of you."

Greta was playing in her playpen, doing all the cute things she usually did, like trying to put her feet in her mouth, but nobody seemed to notice. Everyone was looking at me.

"You've grown up right under our eyes, son," my dad said, petting Grey for a minute. "I guess we didn't even see it happen."

Then everyone got quiet. We all were staring at Grey, who sat in the corner of the living room, cleaning herself as if she belonged there. She rubbed her ears back, wiped her tail and polished it, then took care of her paws. The only sound in the living room was Grey's purring as she took her bath. I stood there waiting for my mom or dad to tell me it was time to take Grey back to Mrs. Beasley's house.

But neither of them said anything. My mom walked over to Grey and stroked her on the back. Finally, she picked up the cat. She looked almost like a little girl herself, standing there hugging Grey. "I guess I forgot how good it feels to hold a cat," she said. Grey let herself be held as if she knew this was a big moment for all of us.

"If Grey belongs to you, then she belongs to us," my mother said. "Isn't that right, Grey?"

My dad took some bits of cheese and put them down on a small plate. "You worked hard today, Grey. Maybe you'd like a snack before dinner."

We told Mrs. Beasley right away that Grey had found a home. Then Grandpop Willie and I went to the supermarket and bought Grey her own red cat dish and a small red water bowl. We bought a kitty litter pan, some kitty litter, and a big brush and comb so that Grey could keep her dignity. That night I went to sleep with Grey tucked around my feet keeping them warm.

Grandpop waited a few days until Mrs. Beasley was up and around, to help her get to where she had to go. She couldn't drive yet, so Grandpop drove her to the post office to pick up the mail. There was a lot of it, and most of the envelopes had checks inside.

"We're going to be fine for the entire year and maybe next year," Mrs. Beasley said. She had some color in her cheeks now and her nurse was gone. "We'll be able to buy plenty of food for our cats. But the best part of all," Mrs. Beasley said to Grandpop and me when we came to visit, "is that there is a big piece of property right off Main Street with plenty of land for the cats to run around, and the township has agreed to let me buy it for quite a reasonable amount of money. When I sell this house, I should have enough to move. There are so many rooms in the house, Jimmy will be able to come with us and live there."

When Grandpop Willie finally left for home, he took two cat carriers with him. One held a red cat, named Fire, and the other a big brown cat that no one had adopted. "He's old, like me," Grandpop said. "We'll get along just fine."

Later that night, after Grandmom Sarah had called long distance to tell us Grandpop had arrived just fine and she loved her two new friends, I went into Greta's bedroom. I didn't go in there very often, but tonight I wondered what she was doing. I thought, since the last few days everyone was interested in me, maybe she was lonely. I knew that didn't feel too good.

When I leaned over her crib, she looked up at me, kicked her feet in the air, and grabbed my hand. I couldn't believe how strong she was. She gave me a big smile as if she knew me. Before I knew it, she was gurgling and baby talking as if she wanted me to stay a while. I guess she didn't like being alone, either.

Then I went into my bedroom. Grey was sitting on my bed, looking very dignified, the way Mrs. Beasley would have liked. She looked over at me, and it was as if I suddenly understood. Grey had decided where *she* would come to live. My parents didn't know it yet, but they really had nothing to say about the matter. Cats are the ones who make important decisions like that.

Until this moment, I thought I had picked out Grey. Sitting there on the bed watching her play, I realized she had picked me. Grey had just waited patiently all these months for me to bring her home.

## About the Author

HARRIET MAY SAVITZ has written many books for young readers, including *Fly, Wheels, Fly!*, which was nominated for the Dorothy Canfield Fisher Memorial Children's Book Award, and *Run, Don't Walk*, which was made into an ABC After School Special. She is also the author of *Swimmer*, another Scholastic Apple Paperback. Ms. Savitz lives in New Jersey.

# America's Favorite Series

## THE BABY-SITTERS Club®

### by Ann M. Martin

**Collect Them All!**

The seven girls at Stoneybrook Middle School get into all kinds of adventures...with school, boys, and, of course, baby-sitting!

| | | |
|---|---|---|
| ☐ MG41128-4 | #14 Hello, Mallory | $2.7 |
| ☐ MG41588-3 | Baby-sitters on Board! Super Special #1 | $2.9 |
| ☐ MG41587-5 | #15 Little Miss Stoneybrook...and Dawn | $2.7 |
| ☐ MG41586-7 | #16 Jessi's Secret Language | $2.7 |
| ☐ MG41585-9 | #17 Mary Anne's Bad-Luck Mystery | $2.7 |
| ☐ MG41584-0 | #18 Stacey's Mistake | $2.7 |
| ☐ MG41583-2 | #19 Claudia and the Bad Joke | $2.7 |
| ☐ MG42004-6 | #20 Kristy and the Walking Disaster | $2.7 |
| ☐ MG42005-4 | #21 Mallory and the Trouble with Twins | $2.7 |
| ☐ MG42006-2 | #22 Jessi Ramsey, Pet-sitter | $2.7 |
| ☐ MG42007-0 | #23 Dawn on the Coast | $2.7 |
| ☐ MG42002-X | #24 Kristy and the Mother's Day Surprise | $2.7 |
| ☐ MG42003-8 | #25 Mary Anne and the Search for Tigger | $2.7 |
| ☐ MG42419-X | Baby-sitters' Summer Vacation Super Special #2 | $2.9 |
| ☐ MG42503-X | #26 Claudia and the Sad Good-bye | $2.9 |
| ☐ MG42502-1 | #27 Jessi and the Superbrat | $2.9 |
| ☐ MG42501-3 | #28 Welcome Back, Stacey! | $2.9 |
| ☐ MG42500-5 | #29 Mallory and the Mystery Diary | $2.9 |
| ☐ MG42499-8 | Baby-sitters' Winter Carnival Super Special #3 (December '89) | $2.9 |

### Available wherever you buy books...or use the coupon below.

Scholastic Inc. P.O. Box 7502, 2932 E. McCarty Street, Jefferson City, MO 65102

Please send me the books I have checked above. I am enclosing $_____
(please add $1.00 to cover shipping and handling). Send check or money order–no cash or C.O.D.'s please.

Name_____

Address_____

City_____ State/Zip_____

Please allow four to six weeks for delivery. Offer good in U.S.A. only. Sorry, mail order not available to residents of Canada.   Prices subject to change.